ISBN
978-0-9856429-3-8
Library of Congress Control Number
2013946972

C IS FOR CHICAGO

Written by Maria Kernahan

Illustrated by Michael Schafbuch

A is for Art Institute where the lions stand proud.

They guard the precious art inside
and welcome the crowd.

B is for Chicago Blues, the sound heard on the street.

Jam with a harmonica and keep time with your feet.

C is for Chicago, Second City and Third Coast.

From the lakefront to the skyscrapers it's a city with the most.

D is for deep dish, Chicago's pizza pie.

It has a thick and buttery crust and cheese piled so high.

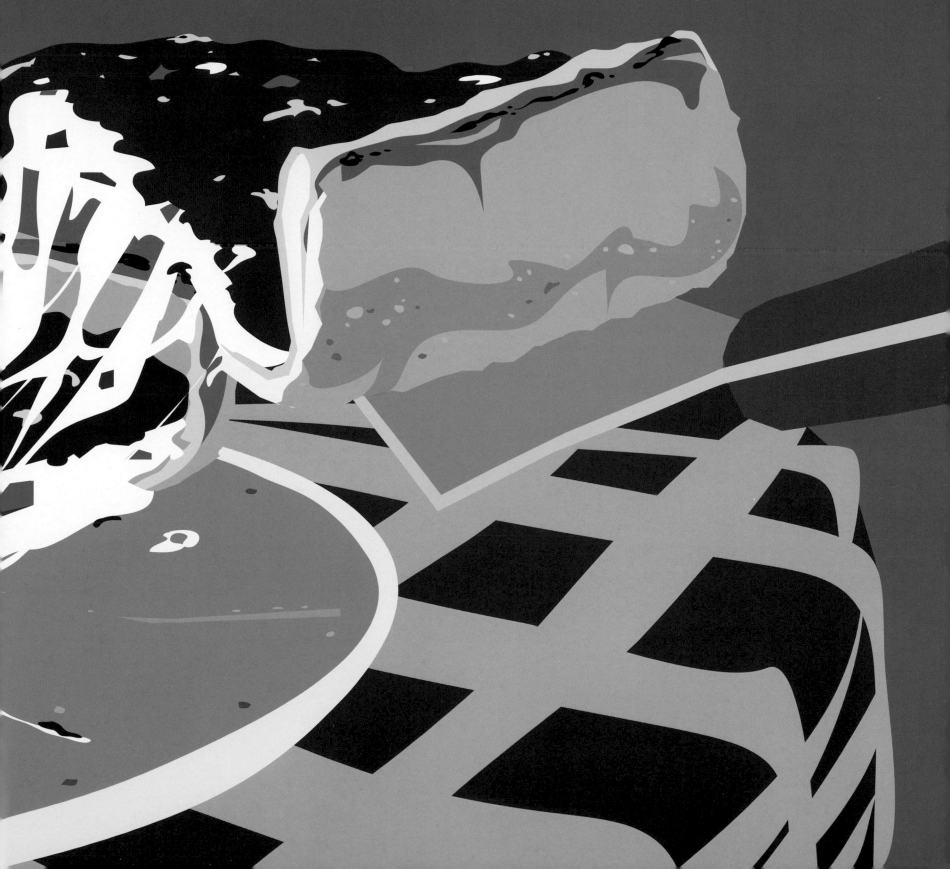

E is for the elevated,
or do you say "the L"?

It loops throughout the city
and goes underground as well.

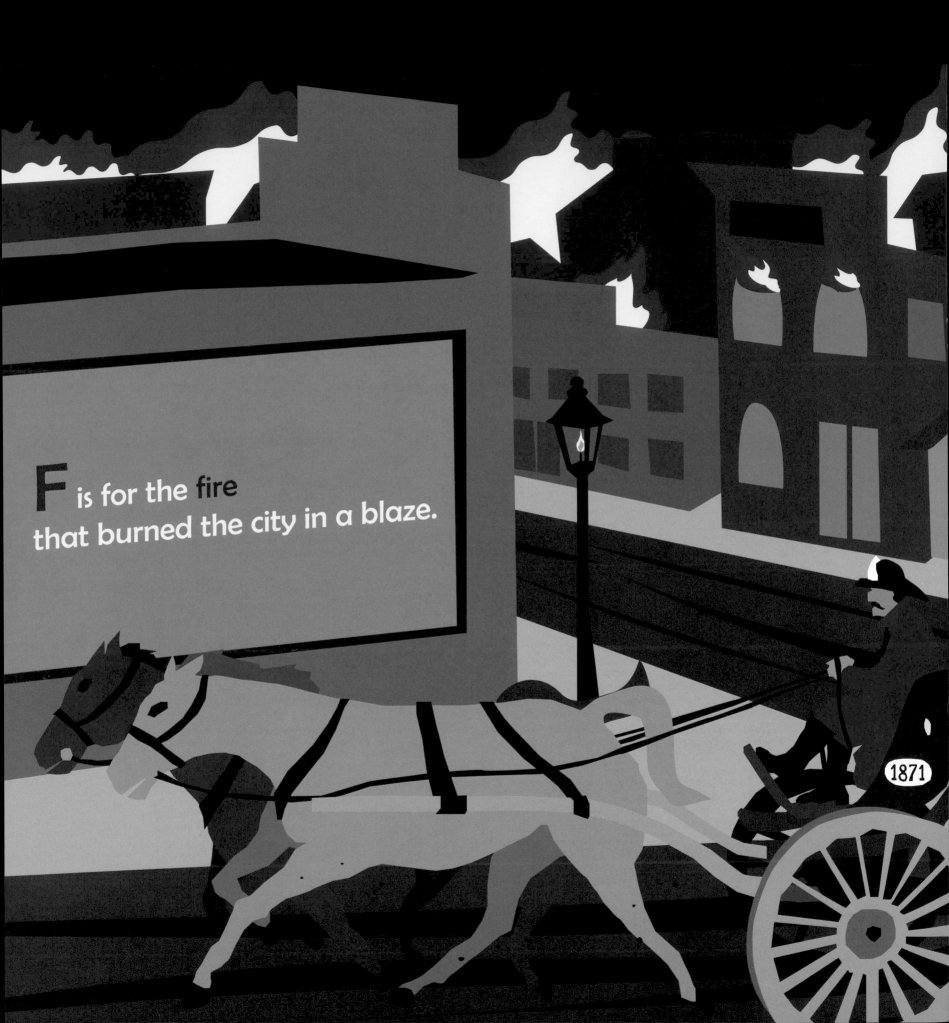

F is for the fire
that burned the city in a blaze.

1871

Started by a naughty cow,
it raged on for three days.

G is for Grant Park where the winds from the lake blow.
It's here that Buckingham Fountain puts on quite a show.

H is for hot dogs on steamed poppy seed buns.

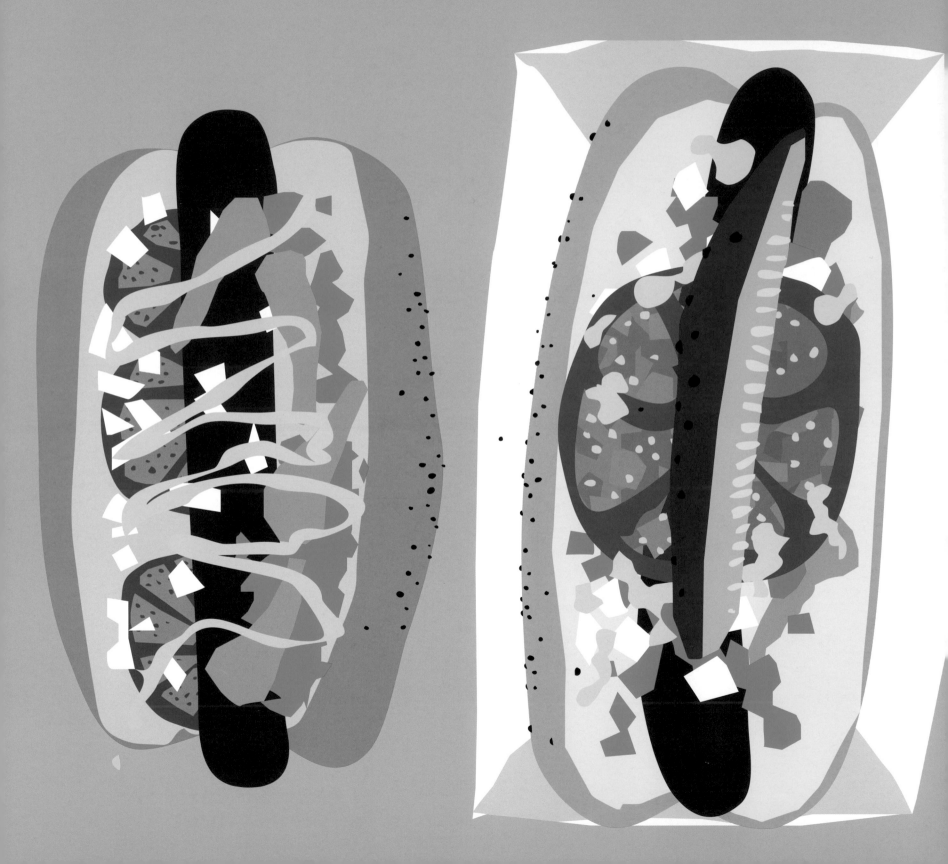

With a garden full of toppings it's hard to eat just one.

I is for the ivy on Wrigley Field's brick wall.

See a game at the ballpark and catch a home run ball.

J is for the jerseys worn by our favorite teams.

Every season we start fresh with championship dreams.

K is for kayaking
under bridges and tall towers.

Zip across the water
using only paddle power.

TAXI

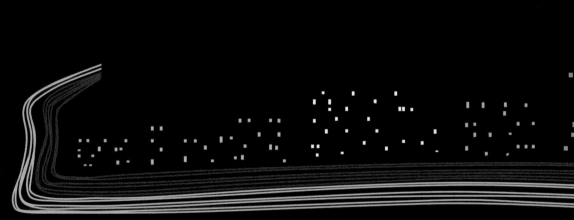

L is for Lake Shore Drive, it zooms next to the lake.
From the South Side to the North Side it's the prettiest route to take.

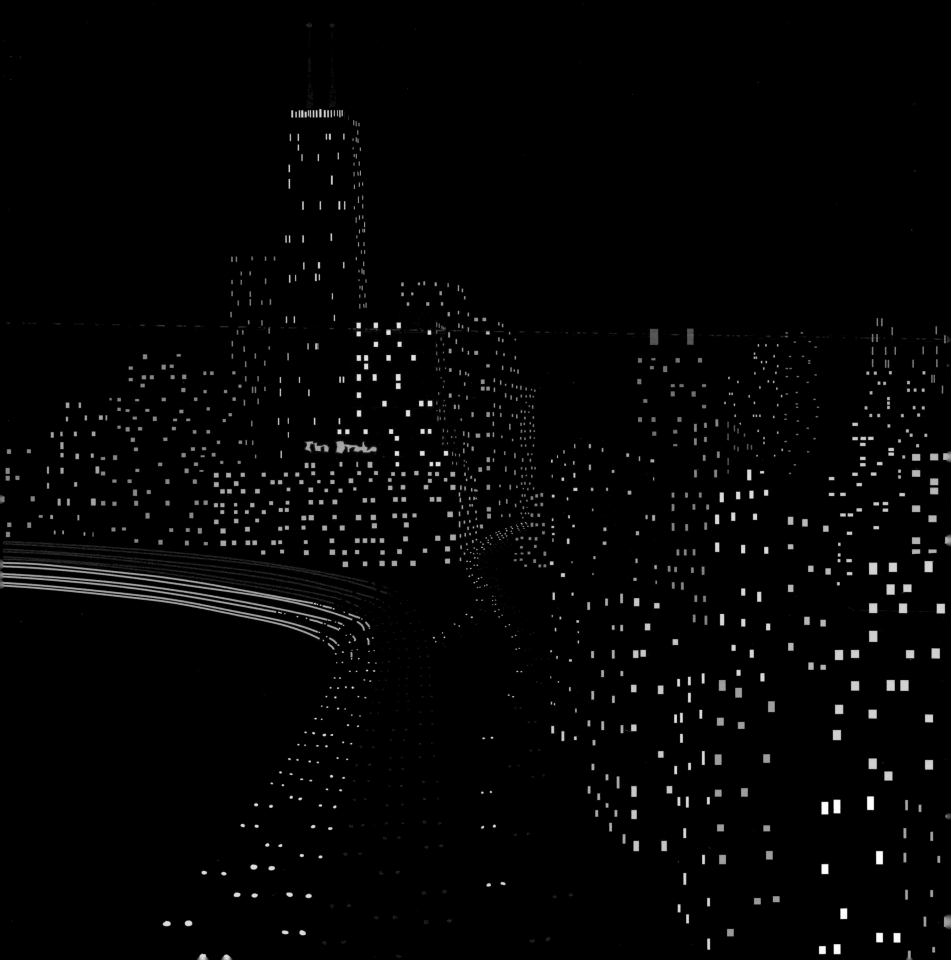

M is for Millennium Park, it's here you'll find "The Bean".

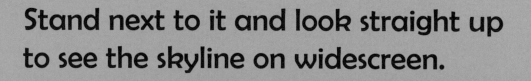

Stand next to it and look straight up
to see the skyline on widescreen.

N is for Navy Pier and all its great attractions.
Ride up in the big Ferris wheel and check out all the action.

O is for Oak Street Beach at the end of the Mag Mile.

Visit on a summer day and you'll want to stay awhile.

P is for the Public Art

that turns our streets into museums.

On plazas
and in public parks,

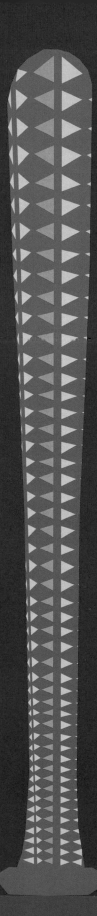

you can't help
but to see 'em.

Q is for the colorful quilt
that's a patchwork of our parts.

Each neighborhood is so unique
but they all capture our hearts.

R is for Chicago River, it flows from east to west.

Once a year on St. Patrick's Day, it wears its Irish best.

S is for Chicago **Softball**, here it's played without a mitt.
The ball is big and squishy, and it's easier to hit.

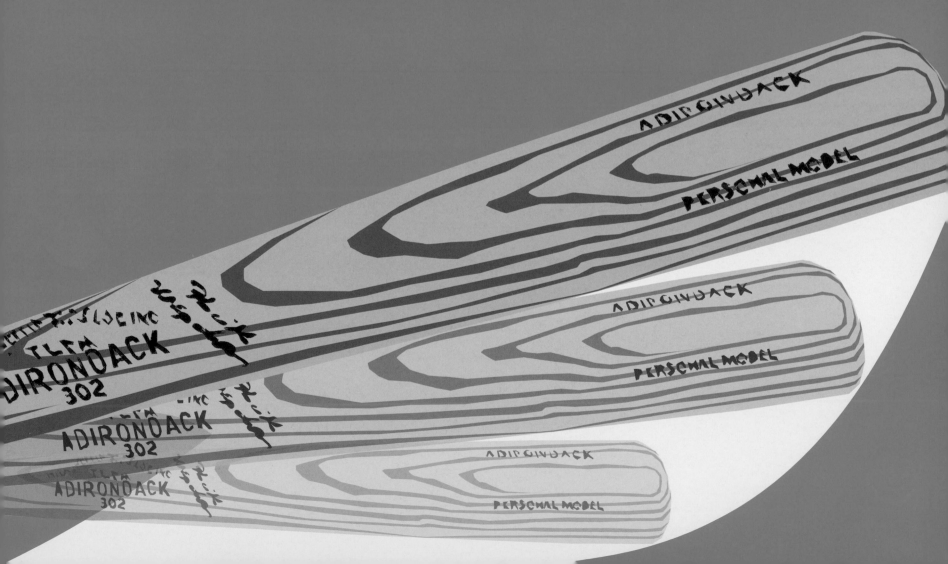

T is for the **T-Rex** who once caused a lot of fright.

Now you can stand next to her since she no longer bites.

U is for U-505, a sub captured in the war.

It was given to Chicago for people to explore.

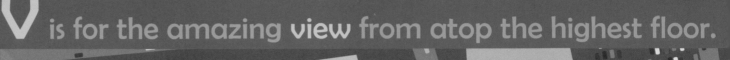

V is for the amazing **view** from atop the highest floor.

W is for the **Water Tower** that survived the Chicago Fire.
It's still standing there today and is something to admire.

X is for the **X's** on the mighty John Hancock. They're bigger on the bottom and smaller at the top.

Y is for the yellow cabs that dart through downtown streets.

They're the best way to get around in the snow and in the sleet.

Z is for the Lincoln Park Zoo, it has a little farm.

The cows and pigs like city living, it has a special charm.

Thank you

T is for **Thank You**, it's not just a letter.
Your help was amazing, it made us much better.

Christopher and Matthew, Meggie, Claire and Libby,
Maureen and Big Daddy.

Thanks to the families that helped by reading early drafts.
We needed the extra eyes, big and little!

The Bemis's
The Gales
The Grables
The Grants
The Johnsons
The McBreens
The Melgards
The Schafbuchs
The Soufers

For the Grandmothers

Patricia Howard "Mumu"
Elizabeth Kernahan "Granny Q"
Susan Schafbuch "Ichi"